OCT 2018

D1467799

LIBBY WIMBLEY

BIRDHOUSE BUILDER

by Amy Cobb illustrated by Alexandria Neonakis

Calico Kid

An Imprint of Magic Wagon
abdopublishing.com

For Delaney, my littlest heart. With special appreciation to Heidi for your kindness and encouragement. —AC

For John, Gooby and Kitty, whose love and support make my career possible. —AN

abdopublishing.com

Published by Magic Wagon, a division of ABDO, PO Box 398166, Minneapolis, Minnesota 55439. Copyright © 2018 by Abdo Consulting Group, Inc. International copyrights reserved in all countries. No part of this book may be reproduced in any form without written permission from the publisher. Calico Kid™ is a trademark and logo of Magic Wagon.

Printed in the United States of America, North Mankato, Minnesota.
052017
092017

Written by Amy Cobb
Illustrated by Alexandria Neonakis
Edited by Heidi M.D. Elston
Art Directed by Laura Mitchell

Publisher's Cataloging in Publication Data

Names: Cobb, Amy, author. | Neonakis, Alexandria, illustrator.
Title: Birdhouse builder / by Amy Cobb ; illustrated by Alexandria Neonakis.
Description: Minneapolis, MN : Magic Wagon, 2018. | Series: Libby Wimbley
Summary: It's a snow day for Libby and Becca! That means making snow angels, sledding, and looking for animal tracks, which leads them to some hungry birds. Libby and Becca decide to help the birds. They build them a tree house to keep them warm and provide snacks so they won't be hungry.
Identifiers: LCCN 2017930832 | ISBN 9781532130236 (lib. bdg.) | ISBN 9781614798507 (ebook) | ISBN 9781614798552 (Read-to-me ebook)
Subjects: LCSH: Birds—Juvenile fiction. | Birdhouses—Juvenile fiction. | Friendship—Juvenile fiction.
Classification: DDC [Fic]—dc23
LC record available at http://lccn.loc.gov/2017930832

Table of Contents

Chapter #1

A Snow Day!

Libby Wimbley hopped out of bed.
She tugged on her favorite sweater.
Then she ran downstairs where Mom
and Dad sat by the fireplace.

"I'm late for school!" Libby cried.

Mom smiled. "It's okay."

"There's no school today, Libby."
Dad smiled, too.

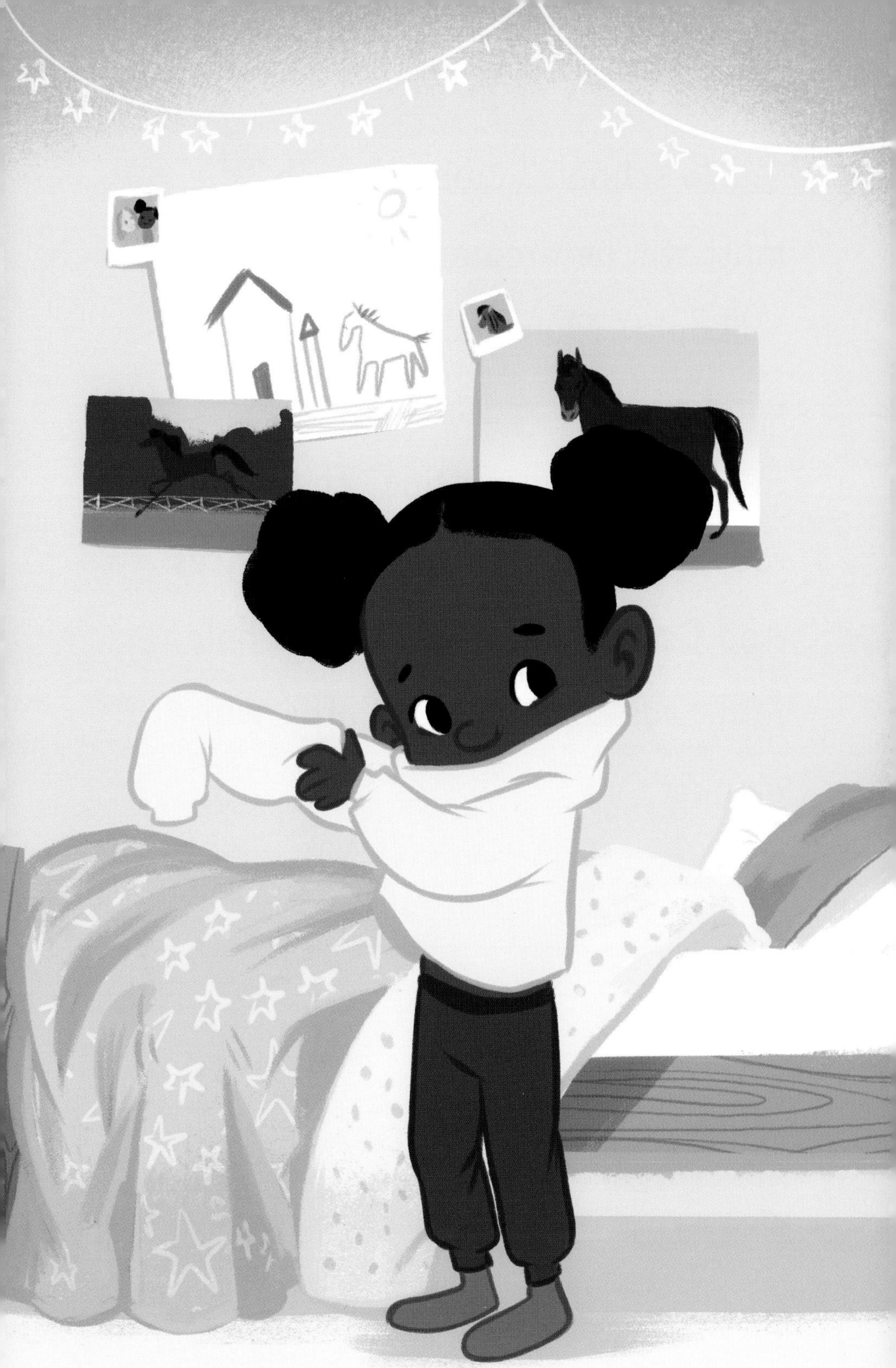

"No school?" Libby thought she must still be dreaming.

"Look!" Mom pointed to the window.

Libby looked outside. The barn roof was white. So were the fences. And Dad's tractor, too. The whole farm was covered in a fluffy, white blanket.

"It snowed!" Libby said, jumping up and down.

"And it's still snowing," Mom said.

"Yay!" Libby cheered. She skipped all around the house, singing, "It's a snow day! It's a snow day! It's a snow day!"

Chapter #2
Hungry Birds

A snow day is made to spend with friends. So Libby's best friend, Becca, came over.

They made snow angels. They built a snow family. And they sledded down the biggest hill on the farm.

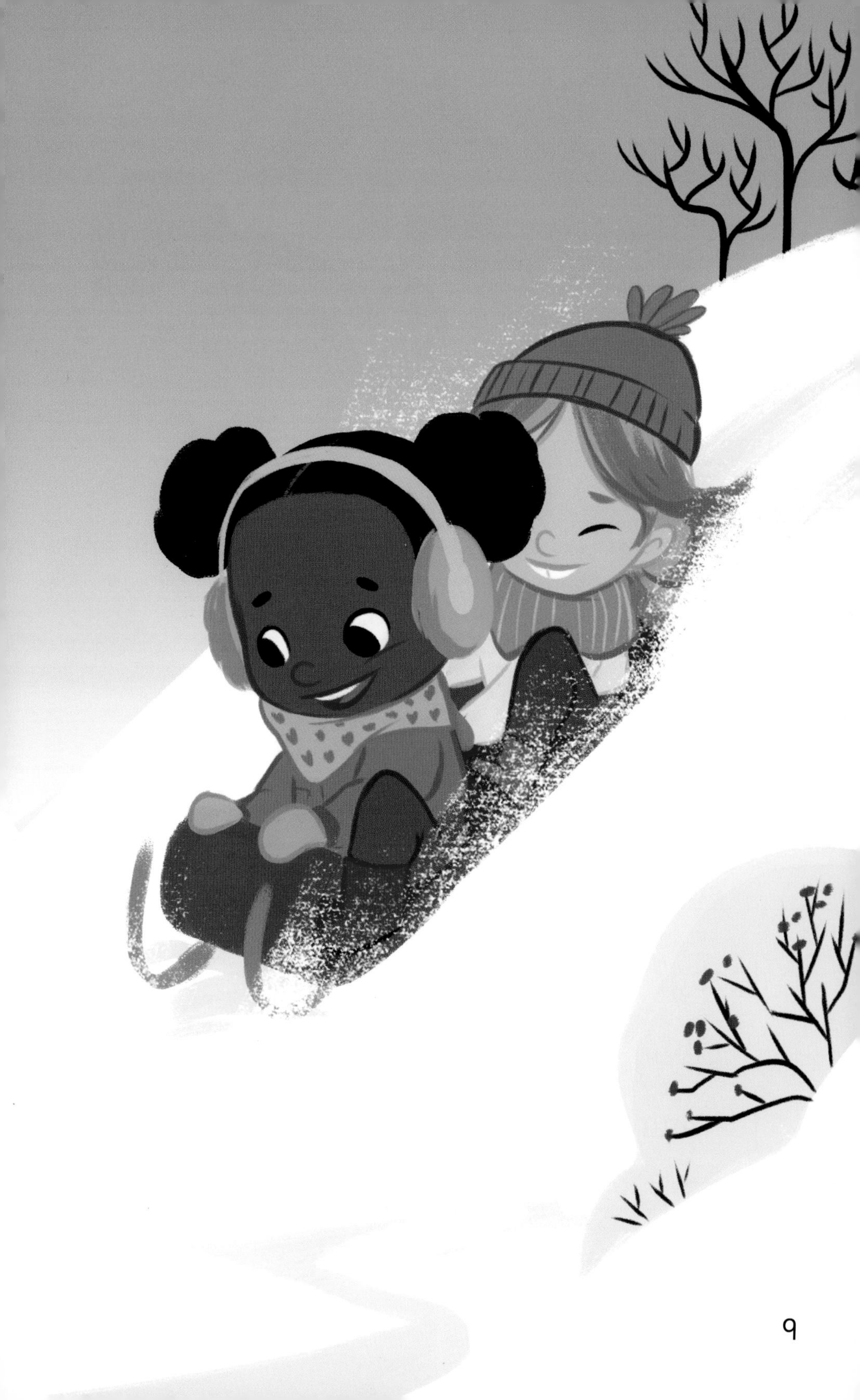

"What do you want to do next,
Libby?" Becca asked.

Libby thought about it. "Let's look
for animal tracks in the snow."

"Cool!" Becca said.

First, Libby spotted a heart-shaped hoofprint. "This one belongs to a deer," she said.

The girls followed it until it disappeared into the forest.

Next, they found a set of rabbit footprints near the path that led to the pond.

Then Becca said, "Libby, check out these footprints!"

Libby took a closer look. Three tiny toes pointed forward. And one longer toe pointed backward.

"These are bird tracks," Libby said.

The girls followed the bird tracks to the tall oak tree in the backyard.

There were red birds. There were blue birds. And there were plump gray snowbirds flitting around the tree's bare branches.

"The birds are hungry," Libby said. "They can't find worms and bugs beneath all of this snow."

"That's sad!" Becca said.

Libby nodded. "I know! Let's go inside and find some snacks for them."

"And snacks for us, too!" Becca said.

"Of course!" Libby smiled.

Chapter 3

A Great Idea

Libby and Becca went inside.

Mom had snacks waiting. There was buttery popcorn. And oatmeal raisin cookies.

"Hot chocolate, too!" Libby said.

Mom handed Libby and Becca a mug. "This will warm you girls up."

"Thank you," they said.

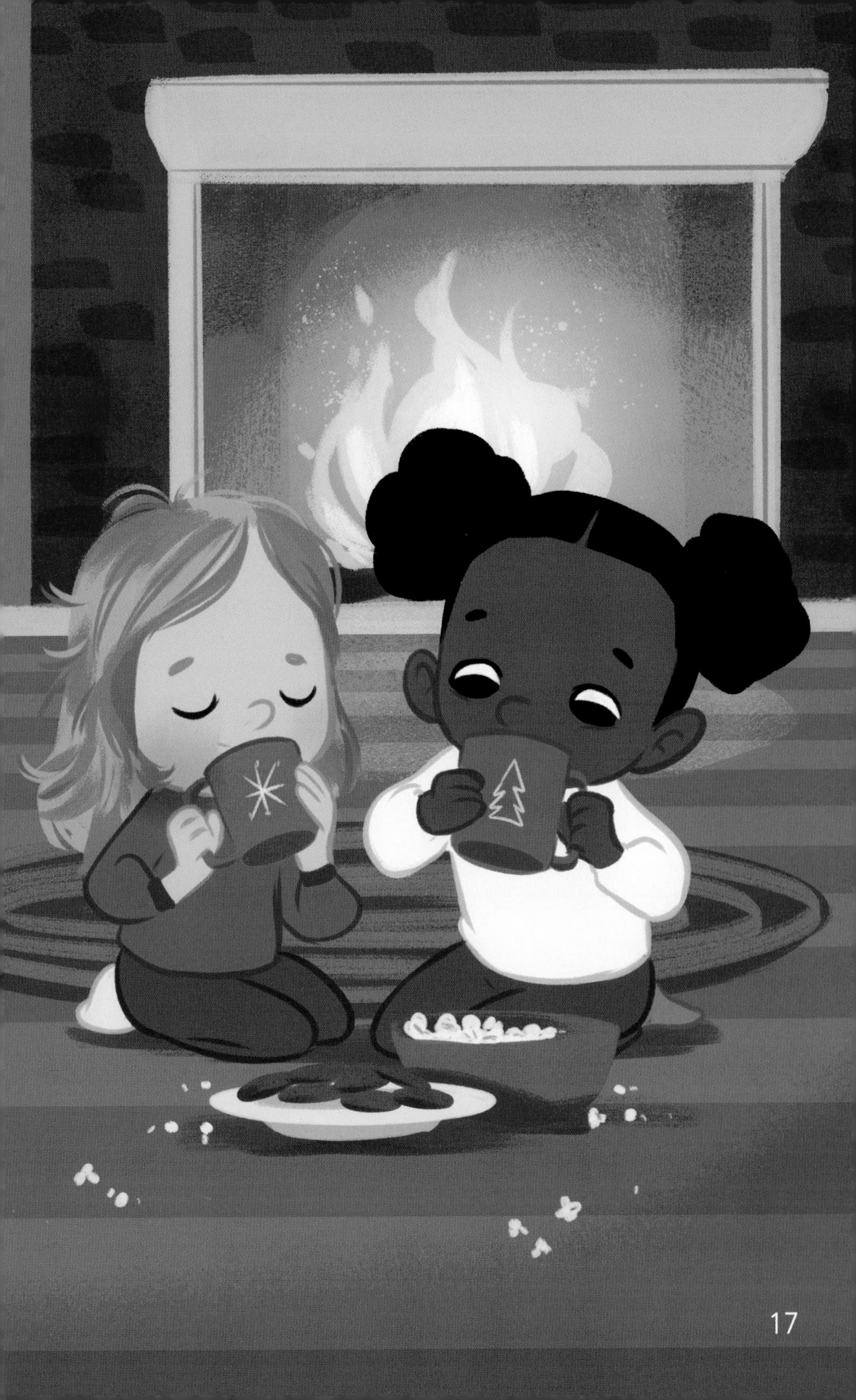

Mom was right. The hot drink did make Libby feel warm.

But Libby still thought about the birds outside. "I wish the birds liked hot chocolate," she said. "Then they wouldn't be cold either."

"We could knit them some tiny scarves," Becca joked.

Libby smiled as she pictured birds wearing fuzzy scarves. But then, Libby thought of a real way to help the birds.

"Becca, let's build the birds a house!" Libby said.

"That's a great idea!" Becca agreed.

Libby could hardly wait to get started.

Chapter 4

Help Wanted

Libby and Becca needed some help.
They found Mom in the kitchen.

"Mom, can you help us build a birdhouse?" Libby asked.

"It'll keep the birds warm," Becca added.

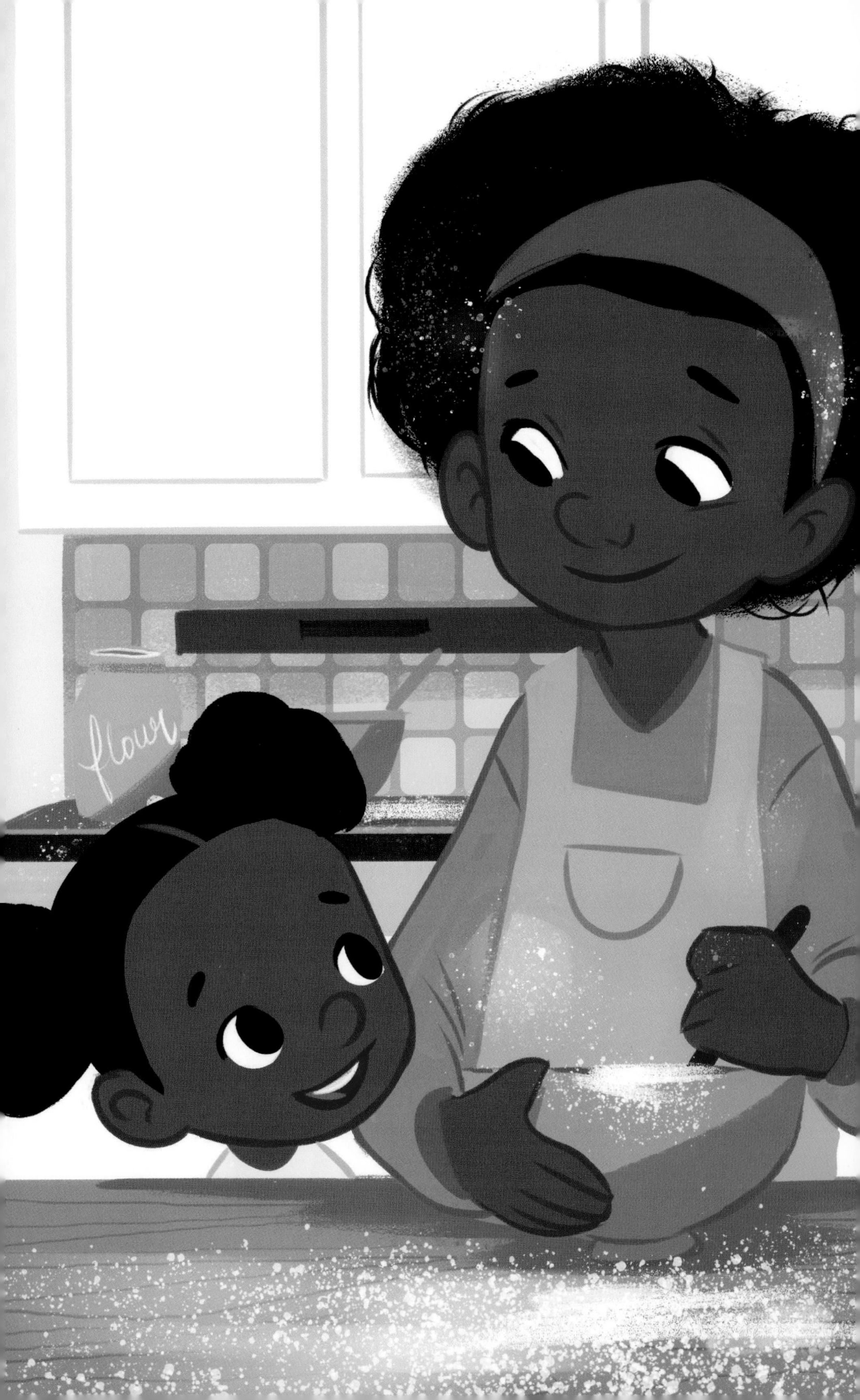
flour

Mom stirred cookie dough. "I'm sorry, girls. I still have more cookies to bake."

"That's okay, Mom," Libby said.

She and Becca slipped back into their coats. Then they headed to the barn.

"Dad, can you help us build a birdhouse?" Libby asked.

"I wish I could," Dad said. "But I'm helping your brother. Stewart and I are making a target for a snowball toss game."

"It's going to be awesome!" Stewart said. "Want to play?"

That did sound like fun.

"Maybe later," Libby said.

She and Becca had a birdhouse
to make. Libby was pretty sure they
could build one on their own.

"We'll need wood," Libby said.

"Don't forget glue," Becca added.

The girls gathered the supplies.
Then they set to work. Before long,
the birdhouse was finished. But it
wasn't very sturdy.

Libby eyed the lopsided birdhouse.
"No bird would want to live here,"
she said sadly.

Chapter #5
Welcome, Birds!

"At least we tried, Libby," Becca said.

Libby knew Becca was right. But she still hoped they could find a way to keep the birds warm.

Then Libby thought of something else. "How about a tree house?"

"Building a tree house sounds even harder," Becca said.

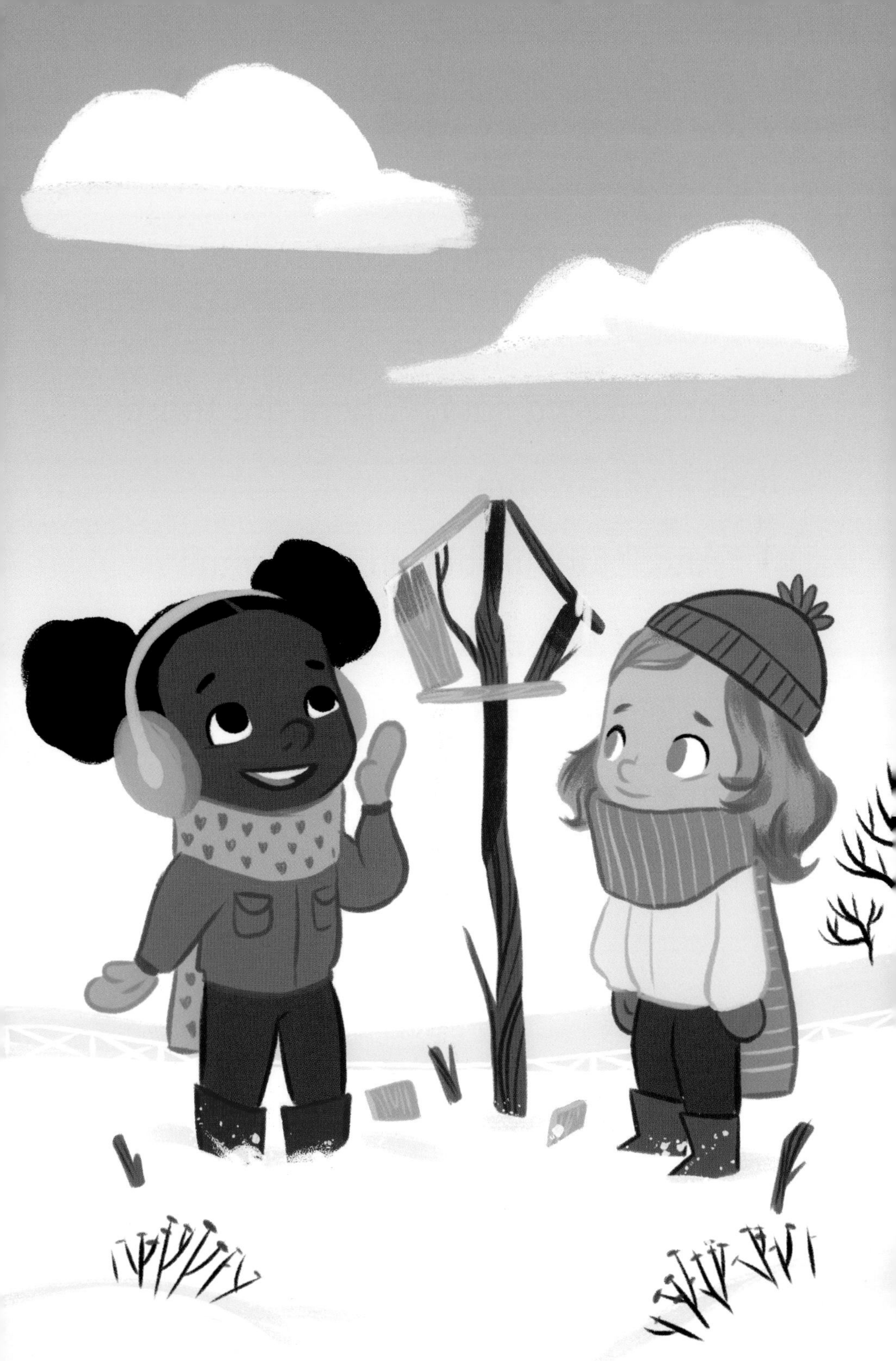

"Right, but I know where there's one already made." Libby smiled. "Follow me!"

Soon, Becca said, "There are those deer tracks again."

"And," Libby pointed to a small evergreen lying on the ground, "there's the tree house! I saw it earlier when we were looking for animal tracks."

The girls dragged the tree home.
They leaned it against the fence. Dad,
Mom, and Stewart gathered around
the tree, too.

"What's this?" Stewart asked.

"It's a tree house for the birds,"
Becca said.

"They can roost inside the branches
to keep warm," Libby added. "We'll
hang snacks on there for them, too."

"Can we help?" Stewart asked.

"Sure!" Libby said.

Mom brought out popcorn and bits of oatmeal raisin cookies.

Libby and Becca dabbed peanut butter on pinecones.

Dad and Stewart tied the tree to the fence, so it wouldn't topple over.

"Wait!" Libby said, running into the barn. She came back with a board from the lopsided birdhouse they'd built earlier. On it, she'd written: Welcome, Birds!

"That's so cute!" Becca said.

"Thanks!" Libby smiled.

Now the birds really did have a perfect winter tree house.

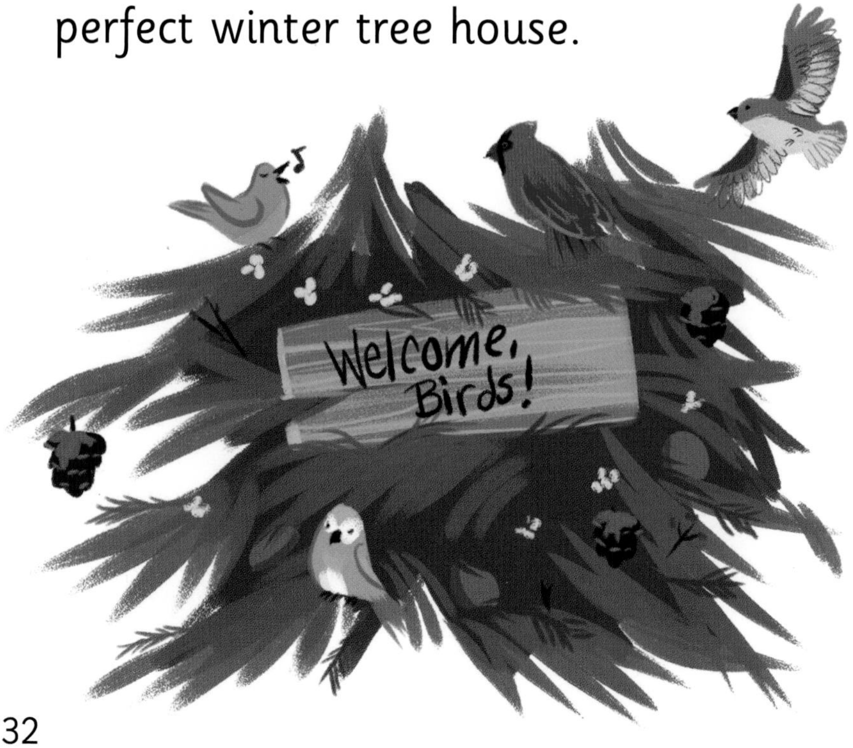
Welcome,
Birds!